KU-512-956

ABOUT A
BEAR

KT 2142844 1

Kingston upon Thames Libraries

KT 2142844 1	
Askews & Holts	30-Apr-2014
JF JFY	£6.99
NM	30029298

For Craig and Honey, you make me
happy and glad every day xx

First published in paperback by HarperCollins Children's Books in 2011

1 3 5 7 9 10 8 6 4 2

ISBN: 978-0-00-741436-9

HarperCollins Children's Books is a division of HarperCollins Publishers Ltd.
Text and illustrations copyright © Holly Surplice 2011
The author/illustrator asserts the moral right to be identified
as the author/illustrator of the work.
A CIP catalogue record for this title is available from the British Library.

All rights reserved.

No part of this publication may be reproduced, stored in a retrieval
system or transmitted in any form or by any means, electronic,
mechanical, recording or otherwise, without the prior permission of
HarperCollins Publishers Ltd, 77-85 Fulham Palace Road,
Hammersmith, London W6 8JB.

Visit our website at: www.harpercollins.co.uk

Printed in China

ABOUT A
BEAR

Holly Surplice

HarperCollins *Children's Books*

A bear can be happy,

A bear can be sad.

A bear can be bored,

And a bear can be glad.

A bear can be puzzled

by a curious find,

And sometimes a bear has to scratch his behind!

A bear can be hungry,
and sniff out a treat.

And
no bear
can
resist
something
sticky
and
sweet.

A bear can be silly,

and do something daft.

But luckily a bear

makes a very good raft!

A bear can get sleepy,

and need a bear hug.

Then cuddle up tight,
as snug as a bug.